BEYOND WORDS

In memory of my loving dad,

JOHN DiCIANNI,

who supported and encouraged me

even though he didn't understand the art world.

Some days I miss you more than words can say.

I lost you way too soon.

I haven't forgotten you,

and I look forward to the day

when we will embrace each other again,

where there will be no more parting. . . .

BEYOND WORDS

*A Treasury of
Paintings and Devotional Writings by*

RON DiCianni

TYNDALE HOUSE PUBLISHERS, INC.
WHEATON, ILLINOIS

In God's sovereignty he raises up unique people for unique
tasks. I feel he has done this with Ron DiCianni. Ron's gifted
skill on canvas is but one of the ways God is using the arts to
show his love. I've met few people who have both the passion
and the ability to do what Ron does. Whether the topic be as
warm as the Prodigal Son or as vivid as spiritual warfare,
Ron brings it to life with palette and brush.

May God use this new work to express what words can't—
but colors can. May you see God's splendor, which indeed
is beyond words.

MAX LUCADO

I've always enjoyed collecting Ltd. Edition prints. But I will never forget the impact the print *Spiritual Warfare* had on my life when I first saw it. My focus changed from just being collector to being a *giver* of prints. I've especially enjoyed seeing the joy and hope *The Prodigal* has brought to many.

MORRIS CHAPMAN

Ron DiCianni is the preacher on canvas. The theme of his art, like that of any great preacher, always focuses on the Cross and redemption. Ron paints and men weep. With God holding Ron's hand, the "old, old story" becomes a dramatic visual theme of glory. Many times I have stood before Ron's work and wept as I have seen myself in each painted character.

KEVIN TURNER,
The Voice of the Martyrs

The purpose of much of the Bible is to turn a seeing eye into a hearing ear. In *Beyond Words* Ron DiCianni does this as well. The images he presents in this powerful book challenge us to hear and understand the message of the Word with our eyes.

MICHAEL CARD

It is always a delight to the eye and food for the soul to turn each page of each new work our Lord creates through Ron DiCianni. It is an example of what God can do when any of His children yield their mind and hand to Him.

MIKE ADKINS,
author of *A Man Called Norman*

I've always enjoyed Ron's work because viewing a DiCianni painting is like having a heart level conversation with him. Putting brush to canvas, he shares his soul, confronts with truth, illuminates with surprises.

FRANK PERETTI

Sometimes truth comes across more clearly with a picture than a page of words. Ron paints the truth, not with his head, but his heart. And the result? We see the love of the Lord more clearly.

JONI EARECKSON TADA

Ron DiCianni's expression through paintings and his illustrated stories have not only inspired me, but have moved me to produce them into film. His insight into the everyday causes us all to look at our world, relationships, and work through different eyes. Without question, Ron is truly a gifted artist. He shares in the vision and commitment of Impact Productions of reaching a sight and sound generation.

TOM NEWMAN,
Impact Productions

The courage and vision that Ron DiCianni has shown over the years in standing as a servant/artist for God and Jesus Christ will always be an inspiration for me. I thank him for answering the call of God to "reclaim the arts for Christ." A more zealous man in the Lord I have rarely met, and this is particularly hard to find in our contemporary art world. I have no doubt that this anointed collection of paintings and devotions will be used in a mighty way by God to build His kingdom.

MICHAEL DUDASH,
artist and illustrator

Visit Tyndale's exciting Web site at www.tyndale.com

If you would like more information about the availability of Ron DiCianni prints, call 1-800-391-1136 or visit Ron DiCianni's Web site at www.art2see.com

Copyright © 1998 by Ron DiCianni. All rights reserved.

Cover illustration © 1998 by Ron DiCianni. All rights reserved.

Designed by Catherine Bergstrom

Edited by Vinita Hampton Wright

Published in association with the literary agency of Alive Communications, Inc., 1465 Kelly Johnson Blvd., Ste. 320, Colorado Springs, CO 80920.

Unless otherwise indicated, all Scripture quotations are taken from the *Holy Bible,* New Living Translation, copyright © 1996. Used by permission of Tyndale House Publishers, Inc., Wheaton, Illinois 60189. All rights reserved.

Scripture quotations marked NIV are taken from the *Holy Bible,* New International Version®. NIV®. Copyright © 1973, 1978, 1984 by International Bible Society. Used by permission of Zondervan Publishing House. All rights reserved.

Scripture quotations marked "NKJV" are taken from the New King James Version. Copyright © 1979, 1980, 1982 by Thomas Nelson, Inc. Used by permission. All rights reserved.

Library of Congress Cataloging-in-Publication Data

DiCianni, Ron.
    Beyond words : a treasury of paintings and devotional writings by / Ron DiCianni
      p.   cm.
    ISBN 0-8423-0176-3 (alk. paper)
    1. Meditations.   I. Title
BV4832.2..D52   1998
242—dc21   98-17526

ISBN 0-8423-0176-3 Hardcover
ISBN 0-8423-0191-7 Deluxe Edition

Printed in Mexico

07 06 05 04 03 02 01 00 99 98
10 9   8   7   6   5   4   3   2

TABLE OF CONTENTS

Acknowledgments ix
A Special Word from the Artist/Author xi

DEVOTIONS
Listed by title of the artwork

In the Beginning 1	The Prodigal 41
The Fall......................................5	The Cleansing Stream 45
Elizabeth's Secret 9	The Touch................................49
The Overshadowing.................13	Into His Presence....................53
Heaven's Loss...........................17	The Chisel 57
Simeon's Moment 21	The Servant 61
The Leper 25	Angels Unseen 65
The Cross.................................29	Spiritual Warfare......................69
Resurrection Morning..............33	The Rapture 73
Mercy 37	Heaven's Door..........................77

A Painter's Story..81

ACKNOWLEDGMENTS

It would be impossible for me to thank every person who has contributed to my life to make it what it is. I can, however, thank those who have worked side by side with me to make this book what it is.

To my partner, Jim Mozdren, for introducing me to Tyndale.

Ron Beers, for taking a giant step of faith. I hope your mustard seed blooms.

Vinita Wright; through your editing you taught me to be a better writer. Thank you.

Cathy Bergstrom; your design ideas were truly inspired.

Meg Diehl, for all you did behind the scenes.

Steve Welch, who always told me "It can be done."

Rick Christian; you were very generous to a novice.

As always, to my wife, Pat, who put her own life on hold many days, attending meetings, adding ideas, and listening patiently to my dreaming. I felt that you were proud of me, even on those really dark days nobody else saw.

Most important, every good thing that came from the Lord to me should point back to Him. I hope this book accomplishes that.

A SPECIAL WORD
FROM THE ARTIST/AUTHOR

This book has undergone a complete transformation since it was first proposed some years ago. This is due to the transformation I have undergone in the interim.

Over the years I have been asked countless times if a compilation of my work and writings would ever be considered. To an artist/author that would be considered enough "market research" to know that such a project would be worth one's time and effort. But that is no longer my motivation for what you are holding in your hands. This is now less a book for your eyes than for your heart.

Not too long ago, I received the kind of news we all fear. The doctors diagnosed me with two blocked coronary arteries. I was devastated. More than that, I was convinced God had left me powerless. My family and I have subsequently traversed what St. John of the Cross called "the dark night of the soul." Everything I thought I knew about God changed and was challenged. He was, seemingly, nowhere to be found. That was pretty discouraging after many years of what I had known as a "close" relationship with my Heavenly Father.

When an artist comes to the realization that the painting he is working on needs some major adjustment to become the masterpiece he envisioned, it's sometimes necessary to scrape off the existing paint and start over. I feel as if my life's forty-five-year-old painting is being restored. I believe it will be even better this time around.

Dear fellow traveler, have you been there? Perhaps you are there now. Is your faith "being sorely tried"? This book, then, may be just for you. In its pages are words and paintings that are meant to help you refocus on the One who said, "I will never fail you. I will never forsake you" (Hebrews 13:5). I hope it will help you discover that He's been sitting right next to you the whole time. That's what we have been finding to be true in our situation; we thought you might be comforted to have hope for yours.

I have often asked God to hold my works in His hands and, like stars, fling them out to those He knows might need them. My sincere desire is that is what just happened to you. May your hurting be wrapped in the nail-pierced hands that were wounded so that you could be healed. May it happen quickly.

Please make good use of the journal on the last page of each section. God is not afraid of your thoughts. He already knows them. In fact, He holds each of your tears in His bottle (Psalm 56:8).

UNLOCKING THE MEANING OF THE ART
People have consistently asked me three questions about my paintings.

"How do your paintings reflect Scripture?"
My aim is to be *metaphorically* accurate. I wish to convey to the viewer the *essence* of the passage I am

illustrating. I am not so much interested in having the viewer relate to the historical information as I am in conveying the dynamic of the Scripture passage being represented.

For instance, when I do a painting that includes an angel, I am trying to get your imagination to focus on the existence of angels in general. I'm not pretending to know what an angel looks like! How would I know? That is of secondary importance to me. If you merely walk away from the painting saying, "Now I know what an angel wing looks like!" the painting hasn't done for you what I'd hoped. I'm going after the *spirit* of the passage. I want you to be moved and changed by the knowledge that God appoints his angels to protect us and do his will.

Certainly, whenever I can also be historically accurate, I will, but that's of less importance in most cases. Sometimes the historical aspect is the purpose for the painting, as in the painting in which I picture Gabriel standing next to the altar of incense. I needed to research exactly what that altar looked like and build a model to exact specifications in order to draw from it. However, in every case, my painting is my *interpretation* of a particular passage or dynamic.

"Are you deliberately trying to hide things in your paintings?"
I have never set out to hide anything in my work. Rather, there are elements of secondary and tertiary importance to the central theme represented in my work. In a painting we lessen the importance of an element by changing its size, color, or rendering. The lesser elements become slightly obscure at that point. When a person "discovers" them later, it can seem that the element was hidden.

This is why it is important to study these paintings. When you think you have the overall theme—after you "get it"—it can be exciting to discover related messages that will expand your appreciation for the things of God.

"Where's the cross in the painting?"
Contrary to what some people have claimed, I do *not* have a cross in every one of my paintings, although there is a cross in many of them. There are several reasons for this. For one, I discovered that people were concentrating on finding the cross in a painting rather than focusing on the central theme of the work. That runs counter to why the painting was done in the first place.

When I have placed a cross in the painting, it is to bring us back to this all-encompassing fact: Without Christ, we are hopeless. Many times I have heard people use phrases like "trust in God" or "have faith in God." You can have all the trust or faith in the world, but without Christ we have no access to God. This isn't a matter of my artistic interpretation; it's His word (John 14:6). While it is my aim to always point to Christ, the paintings can do that at times without using the symbol of the cross.

CREATION

IN THE BEGINNING
GOD CREATED
THE HEAVENS AND
THE EARTH.
THE EARTH WAS EMPTY,
A FORMLESS MASS
CLOAKED IN DARKNESS.
AND THE SPIRIT OF GOD
WAS HOVERING
OVER ITS SURFACE.

Genesis 1:1-2

In the Beginning

"the p

"petual work of thy creation"

William Cullen Bryant

I once said to Max Lucado that I wished I could impress on my kids that God made everything, including—no, *especially*—them. Max answered, "Tell them that the same hands that made the stars made them." That sure puts things in proper perspective, don't you think?

If you look closely at the stars in this painting, you will see little babies in them. They represent my personal conviction that God knows the name of every aborted baby. "Lift your eyes and look to the heavens: Who created all these? He who brings out the starry host one by one, and calls them each by name" (Isaiah 40:26, NIV). Surely if He knows the stars by name, He knows His children even more intimately!

This concept hit home dramatically for our family when our son Warren was on a high-level soccer team. One night I found him in his room, tearfully curled up on the bed. He'd been subjected to some verbal thrashing by his coach that day. I pointed to the original three-by-four painting of *In the Beginning*, which hangs on the wall above his bed.

We talked of Warren's worth being determined by who he is—God's creation, formed by God's own hands. Warren was a masterpiece, whether or not he met his coach's harsh standard. This was incredibly eye-opening to my son, and I believe it has had a lasting impact on his self-worth. I painted this piece to describe how unique and beautiful each person is to God. I hadn't realized how important it would become to my own child. You may have a child, too, who could use such a reminder.

PAINTER'S NOTES: *The hand of God is lifting Adam from the dust, while Adam's outstretched arms form the shape of the cross. The Scripture says mist covered the ground. I took the liberty of having night and day happen at the same time. A rainbow of birds flies across the hand of God; in his palm, a red bird signifies the nail print in Christ's hand. Even at Creation, God knew that His only Son would die in order to save us and all of creation.*

My heart is awed within me when I think
Of the great miracle that still goes on,
In silence, round me—the perpetual work
Of thy creation, finished, yet renewed forever.
Written on thy works I read
The lesson of thy own eternity.

WILLIAM CULLEN BRYANT (1794–1878)

THOUGHTS FROM THE HEART:

_____

_____

_____

_____

_____

_____

_____

_____

THE FALL

FOR THE WAGES OF SIN
IS DEATH, BUT THE
FREE GIFT OF GOD
IS ETERNAL LIFE
THROUGH CHRIST JESUS
OUR LORD.

Romans 6:23

The Fall

"sin n

...eans breaking God's heart"

— William Barclay

Someone once said, "Almost everyone knows the difference between right and wrong; some people just have to make decisions."

Never was this truer than in the case of Adam and Eve. The God who made them and fellowshipped with them instructed, "You may freely eat any fruit in the garden except fruit from the tree of the knowledge of good and evil. If you eat of its fruit, you will surely die" (Genesis 2:16-17). Decisions, decisions. They opted to disobey their Father's instructions. The rest has become our history.

While Adam and Eve didn't have a "manual" at their crucial moment of decision, we do: the Bible. Yet we choose to ignore what is *best* for what we humanly see as *good*. Like that couple in the Garden, we are without excuse. And we are not without the consequences. To deliberately disobey what God has told us will always end in regret. We need to know the truth—and obey it.

Ultimately, disobedience (sin) hurts not only the perpetrator. It hurts the heart of the Father, whose way is far better than what we settle for. The tragedy is that this kind of "fall" is totally avoidable. That's why God chose to warn us through this written record (1 Corinthians 10:11).

The Fall is described in Genesis 3, a chapter that I think is especially sad for God. The crown of His creation—the man and woman with whom He had shared such intimacy—had to be removed from their place of peace and fellowship with Him.

PAINTER'S NOTES: *I put footprints at the bottom of the painting signifying Adam and Eve leaving the Garden. A strong angel (cherubim) is blocking the Garden's entrance with a flaming sword, which flashes back and forth, independent of the angel, ensuring that the fallen will not be able to return to the Garden. I put foliage, birds, and flowers in the background, showing how beautiful the Garden must have been. When adding the waterfalls, I felt inspired to show them coming from God's eyes.*

Sin becomes a crime, not against law, but against love; it means not breaking God's law so much as breaking God's heart.

WILLIAM BARCLAY (1907–1978)

THOUGHTS FROM THE HEART:

_____

_____

_____

_____

_____

_____

_____

_____

_____

PROMISES

> SOON AFTERWARD
> HIS WIFE, ELIZABETH,
> BECAME PREGNANT AND
> WENT INTO SECLUSION
> FOR FIVE MONTHS.
>
> *Luke 1:24*

Elizabeth's Secret

"the m

"...a mystery I cannot comprehend"

Susanna Wesley

The Bible records that Zechariah doubted God's plan, even though the angel Gabriel appeared to Zechariah personally and told him that his wife, Elizabeth, would give birth to a son. There is no mention of Elizabeth receiving any such special announcement. And, because Zechariah refused to believe Gabriel, he was struck dumb and couldn't have been much help delivering this exciting news to his wife. She had to go entirely on faith, just like the rest of us!

In Luke 1:24 we see that Elizabeth's faith was rewarded; she became pregnant with John shortly after Zechariah returned home. Elizabeth remained in seclusion for five months after that. We are not told why, and we don't know what her thoughts were during that time. Maybe she wanted to take extra care, considering her age (she was past childbearing years), or maybe physical complications kept her off her feet. One thing is for sure: She was preparing for the birth of the forerunner of the Messiah. It must have consumed her every waking moment.

I've tried to capture one of those moments—perhaps when some groceries were brought to the house for meals. Each daily routine must have taken on new significance for Elizabeth. For a few moments the curtains of eternity had slipped back to reveal God's astounding plan. I would guess Elizabeth cherished every thought or reminder of what was happening to her.

PAINTER'S NOTES: *I show a basket of bread and fruit—significant symbols in the Bible—for the fruit of the Spirit and the Bread of Life. The fruit basket casts a shadow on the wall that takes the shape of a baby—the baby who took away Elizabeth's disgrace. This baby, John, would one day look into the eyes of Jesus as he baptized Him in the Jordan River.*

May I adore the mystery I cannot comprehend. Help me to be not too curious in prying into those secret things that are known only to thee, O God, nor too rash in censuring what I do not understand.

SUSANNA WESLEY (1670–1742)

THOUGHTS FROM THE HEART:

_____

_____

_____

_____

_____

_____

_____

_____

_____

CHOSEN

"DON'T BE FRIGHTENED, MARY," THE ANGEL TOLD HER, "FOR GOD HAS DECIDED TO BLESS YOU!"

Luke 1:30

The Overshadowing

"*open*

...my hands to willingly accept"

— Catherine Marshall

At this moment you may be the parent of a teenager or perhaps you are a teenager yourself. With two teenagers of my own, I'm being reminded that these years can be quite perplexing and interesting. Day-to-day changes accompanied by all the insecurities of the future can make it a scary time. Sometimes parents forget that, since we are no longer in these struggles.

With that in mind, consider Mary, possibly the most courageous teen of all time. She did more than take on human responsibilities. She took in the very Son of God. Some speculate her age to have been between twelve and fourteen years. Think you could have handled what was asked of her? Someone remarked once, "He who lacks courage thinks with his legs." Mary probably considered running away. I'm sure a million "no way's" crossed her mind in a split second. Yet her response was, "I am the Lord's servant. May it be to me as you have said" (Luke 1:38, NIV). She was rewarded by carrying the One who would eventually save her.

- - - - -

PAINTER'S NOTES: *The star represents Christ conceived in Mary (the "bright morning star" in Revelation 22:16). I put Mary in a submissive pose, arms clenched to her chest, eyes closed, to signify the incredible insecurity —and wonder—of meeting with holiness. The pot and Mary's robe were initially only props to date the scene. But I was struck with the idea of space, stars, and the heavens in her blue wrap. For the Eternal One had just become part of Mary and would be the salvation of the world. The pot represents Mary as the humble vessel of the Lord who would carry this eternal treasure. The shadow of the dove at her knees identifies the messenger, the Holy Spirit.*

Acceptance says, "This is my situation at the moment. I'll look unblinkingly at the reality of it. But I'll also open my hands to willingly accept whatever a loving Father sends."

CATHERINE MARSHALL (1915–1983)

THOUGHTS FROM THE HEART:

_____
_____
_____
_____
_____
_____
_____
_____
_____

NATIVITY

HE MADE HIMSELF
NOTHING; HE TOOK
THE HUMBLE POSITION
OF A SLAVE
AND APPEARED IN
HUMAN FORM.

Philippians 2:7

Heaven's Loss

"He

...ame into our condition," — John Bunyan

The Nativity has been painted by countless artists. Most of them portray what I would call a romantic version of that event, a version closer to what we want to believe than what actually occurred. No one (not even Mary and Joseph) could have grasped the significance of this birth—except perhaps the unseen visitors who stood by in awesome vigil.

I can only imagine the reaction of an angel, seeing the Lord of all the universe suddenly reduced to a human infant. Surely this night was the most joyous in earth's history—but for whom? Isaiah prophesied hundreds of years earlier that Christ would be "disfigured beyond that of any man and his form marred beyond human likeness" (Isaiah 52:14, NIV). The angels' joy on the night of Christ's birth was different from what we usually think of as joy—they knew how he would suffer and what his life meant ultimately for fallen humanity.

Nearly everyone loves the Christmas story about the baby, but few are willing to face the man on the cross. Christ was not born for Christmas; He was born for Easter! That's why I put a lamb at the foot of the trough. As John would someday exclaim, "Look, the Lamb of God, who takes away the sin of the world!" (John 1:29, NIV).

If we could get a true glimpse of Christmas, we would swallow hard at the reality of what Christ began on that starry night. It is summed up in Hebrews 12:2: "Let us fix our eyes on Jesus, the author and perfecter of our faith, who for the joy set before him endured the cross, scorning its shame, and sat down at the right hand of the throne of God" (NIV). Something to remember the next time we sing "Silent Night."

*Christ did not only come into our flesh,
but also into our condition, into the valley
and shadow of death, where we were,
and where we are, as we are sinners.*

JOHN BUNYAN (1628–1688)

THOUGHTS FROM THE HEART:

_____

_____

_____

_____

_____

_____

_____

_____

PROPHECY

"I HAVE SEEN
THE SAVIOR
YOU HAVE GIVEN TO
ALL PEOPLE.
HE IS A LIGHT
TO REVEAL GOD
TO THE NATIONS,
AND HE IS THE GLORY
OF YOUR PEOPLE
ISRAEL!"

Luke 2:30-32

Simeon's Moment

"the

"...prophets wanted to know"

Peter the Apostle

Imagine holding the very Son of God in your arms—understanding who He is and what he has come to accomplish! When Simeon held the baby Christ, he brought to that experience the centuries of prophecy he had studied and memorized. Simeon remembered God's promises throughout Israel's history—to bring healing and forgiveness. To give them a future and a hope. And now Simeon held the baby who was the fulfillment of all those promises. This moment must have been to Simeon the culmination of his whole lifetime of waiting and hoping. The baby in his arms must have finally satisfied Simeon's deepest heart desires.

Because of what his eyes saw and his hands felt, Simeon was content, ready to leave this life and go to his God. We can only guess (I like to do that at times) what must have raced through Simeon's mind at that moment. He didn't have long to hold the child—but it was long enough to realize that Messiah had come.

PAINTER'S NOTES: *I tried to let Simeon's face tell the story. I have a feeling Simeon embraced that baby as he had embraced nothing else. He knew that he held the Light of the World—note the star emanating from the baby. Intertwined through them both is a map of the world—which Christ came to redeem. (Most people at that time would have thought he had only come for the Jews.) Many of those lands, such as North and South America, were not even known to Simeon's world, but God knew all along that you and I would need a Savior. I added Simeon's tear to reflect deep joy. Upon further contemplation, I realized it could also symbolize Simeon's knowledge of what this baby's future held.*

This salvation was something the prophets wanted to know more about. They prophesied about this gracious salvation prepared for you, even though they had many questions as to what it all could mean.

PETER THE APOSTLE (1 PETER 1:10)

THOUGHTS FROM THE HEART:

_____
_____
_____
_____
_____
_____
_____
_____
_____

HEALING

A MAN WITH LEPROSY
CAME AND KNELT
IN FRONT OF JESUS,
BEGGING TO BE HEALED.
"IF YOU WANT TO,
YOU CAN MAKE ME WELL
AGAIN," HE SAID.
MOVED WITH PITY,
JESUS TOUCHED HIM.
"I WANT TO," HE SAID.
"BE HEALED!"

Mark 1:40-41

The Leper

"on

"...the spirit is healed"

Calvin Miller

This simple story of a few verses has much to tell us. When the leper came to Christ, *he fell on his knees.* Pretty smart guy! He knew he had no bargaining power and assumed the only position left to him. His need showed him that the Saviour was his only hope. How different from the prevailing attitudes in our world today. Often our sense of false security or importance prevents us from taking that humble position before the Lord.

Then the leper "implored" Jesus (NKJV). This term actually refers to one asking as an *inferior of a superior!* This man knew that Jesus was his superior. If only we could realize our utter dependence on the Savior instead of shaking a defiant fist in God's face.

What did the Savior do? He gave the answer every needy person longs to hear. The only One who *can* restore us said, "I am willing" (NIV). And then Jesus did the unthinkable for the Highest of all Priests: *He touched the leper.* Religious law called lepers "unclean," and this dreaded disease was believed to be highly contagious. This was no obstacle for the One who is the "Sun of Righteousness... with healing in his wings" (Malachi 4:2).

For me, this story raises some obvious questions. Can Jesus still heal today, and is He still willing? In my studio I've hung a magnet my son Warren made in Sunday school. In his six-year-old's handwriting he wrote "Jesus heals." I put that magnet where I can see it often to remind myself of healing experiences in our family. We can certainly say that *yes,* Jesus still heals, and *yes* He is willing!

• • • • •

PAINTER'S NOTES: *I avoided showing Christ's face because it is the* spirit *of Christ—beyond historical facts—that I wanted to represent. The little stars appearing at Christ's touch herald the moment of healing. The healed hand is a different color from the other hand, as the healing begins to travel throughout the man's body. The clouds in back of Jesus are beginning to spread and form a cross, a reminder of the price paid for this leper's healing. The small spray of flowers springing from the hard ground is symbolic of the new life emerging from the leper's diseased body.*

Our Father yet heals the spirit of amputees—even when they will not grow legs. And, once the spirit is healed, the legs can be done without.

CALVIN MILLER (1936–)

THOUGHTS FROM THE HEART:

_____
_____
_____
_____
_____
_____
_____
_____

GUILTY

HE CAME ONCE
FOR ALL TIME . . .
TO REMOVE THE
POWER OF SIN FOREVER
BY HIS
SACRIFICIAL DEATH
FOR US.

Hebrews 9:26

The Cross

"favor

...through the Cross of Christ"

Oswald Chambers

I have often wondered who was assigned the task of actually nailing Christ to the cross. What was his name, and what did he look like? How old was he? Was he reluctant to do it, or was it simply another command to be obeyed? Did he realize, shortly after, as the centurion did, that "surely this man was innocent" (Luke 23:47)? Did he repent?

It occurs to me that I know that man intimately. It was me. In fact, I believe that it is not possible to become a Christian until the devastating realization hits you that *you* are responsible for putting Christ there on the cross (Hebrews 10:1-8).

If you see *yourself* in this painting, what is your reaction? You may turn and walk away. Or you may turn to Him and fall on your knees in grateful repentance. Many believe in a God of love, and so He is. But He is also God of justice. And justice, in our case, demands a guilty verdict. Before you entertain the thought that God is too loving and "good" to hold you responsible for neglecting the price His Son paid, remember His justice.

Psalm 32:2 has some great news to consider: "Blessed is the man whose sin the Lord does not count against him" (NIV). Tragedy turns to triumph when we turn *to* the Cross. That is a message important enough—life-changing enough—to tell the whole world!

PAINTER'S NOTES: *I placed myself at the cross. A solitary figure. No one else is to blame. The evidence of the hammer and nails is incriminating proof of my responsibility. All that's left is to fall on the mercy of God. The sky turns dark, stars come out, all nature writhes in pain at their Creator's agony. I have the sun setting, which represents hope fading. Lightning thunders the dreadful news.*

To base our forgiveness on any other ground is unconscious blasphemy. The only ground on which God can forgive our sin and reinstate us to His favor is through the Cross of Christ.

OSWALD CHAMBERS (1874–1917)

THOUGHTS FROM THE HEART:

_____
_____
_____
_____
_____
_____
_____
_____

RESURRECTION

> SUDDENLY THERE WAS A GREAT EARTHQUAKE, BECAUSE AN ANGEL OF THE LORD CAME DOWN FROM HEAVEN AND ROLLED ASIDE THE STONE AND SAT ON IT. . . . "I KNOW YOU ARE LOOKING FOR JESUS, WHO WAS CRUCIFIED. HE ISN'T HERE! HE HAS BEEN RAISED FROM THE DEAD."
>
> *Matthew 28:2-6*

Resurrection Morning

"Res

...rection explains the gospels"

— John S. Whale

What must have been the thoughts of the guards on duty that night? Was it just another night's pay? "See ya, dear. I've got night duty tonight. Ah, just another guy who tried to be a hero. Should be an easy watch...."

Little did they care about the man in the tomb while all of Heaven watched the Holy Spirit gently nudge Christ's shoulder. It was time for the most pivotal act in human history. Jesus Christ had been born for the purpose of this dark night. I can see all in heaven's balconies, poised at attention, to see what had been planned from the beginning. What expectation there must have been. Any disinterested angels? I doubt it! Just apathetic guards.

Before we are too hard on those guards, we should ask ourselves how many times we have missed life's important moments. I'm notorious for looking in the wrong direction or, worse yet, not looking at all while God is about to do something spectacular.

What a lesson there is for us in this scene. First Thessalonians 5:6 reminds us, "So then, let us not be like others, who are asleep, but let us be alert and self-controlled" (NIV).

PAINTER'S NOTES: *The shadow of the cross falls across the stone—an ever-present reminder of the price that was paid for us. The rays of light beginning to emerge from the crack between the stone and the tomb's entrance are my interpretation of that incredible moment when the Light of the World shined once again in a darkened world. That light could not be extinguished. At the top of the painting, the dove, symbol for the Holy Spirit, has done His work in awakening the Prince from His sleep. The long night was over, and Christ's journey into my life, which led Him through the tomb, had begun.*

The Gospels do not explain the Resurrection; the Resurrection explains the Gospels. Belief in the Resurrection is not an appendage to the Christian faith; it is the Christian faith. — JOHN S. WHALE

THOUGHTS FROM THE HEART:

_____
_____
_____
_____
_____
_____
_____
_____

MERCY

"WHERE ARE YOUR
ACCUSERS? DIDN'T
EVEN ONE OF THEM
CONDEMN YOU?"
"NO, LORD," SHE SAID.
AND JESUS SAID,
"NEITHER DO I.
GO AND SIN NO MORE."

John 8:10-11

"me

Mercy

"...cy imitates God"

St. John Chrysostom

Christ's actions often stun and amaze us. An angry crowd demands His decision concerning a woman charged with adultery. Caught in the act, they say. According to religious law, she deserves death.

What does Jesus do? Writes on the ground. Wouldn't you love to know what He wrote? I wonder if the crowd paused to find out, or if they were so bent on the woman's destruction that they looked right past Jesus' words in the dust.

Whatever Jesus wrote, His thinking was the exact opposite of everyone's expectations. Instead of delivering the "inevitable" punishment, Jesus gave a verdict of "guilty, but pardoned" (my translation). Come to think of it, that is my verdict as well.

We may not immediately relate to this story. People today don't get dragged into our neighborhood streets to be stoned to death for this or any other sin. But we understand what it means to be guilty of at least one sin, and one sin against God is enough to render us *guilty*.

I play Monopoly with my kids, and we're always happy to draw that "Get out of jail free" card. Two thousand years have passed, and our Savior is still passing out the "Get out of jail free" cards. Have you accepted that divine gift?

• • • • •

PAINTER'S NOTES: *This painting's simple background helps us focus on the woman and her Savior. She looks up hesitantly, wondering if Jesus' opinion will be any different from her accusers'. Her disheveled hair and garments give some clues to her lifestyle. The shadow of the Savior falls gently upon her. He offers the hopeful message: Get up and try it again. You get a second chance. Notice the dropped rocks that have fallen to form the shape of the cross. At this time, the woman wouldn't understand what that symbol would later mean to her and all people. But we know the rest of the story—that this woman, like us, could be forgiven because Christ gave His life on the cross. She got the benefit early!*

Mercy imitates God and disappoints Satan.

ST. JOHN CHRYSOSTOM (C. 347–407)

THOUGHTS FROM THE HEART:

_____

_____

_____

_____

_____

_____

_____

_____

RETURNING

THERE IS JOY IN THE PRESENCE OF GOD'S ANGELS WHEN EVEN ONE SINNER REPENTS.

Luke 15:10

The Prodigal

"Jesu

"...ready stands to save you"

Joseph Hart

The universal appeal of this painting has made it one of my favorites. The continued reactions I see from people confirm that Luke 15 is as relevant today as when Jesus first told the story. This scene of a father accepting his son, just as he is, happens every day—spiritually, that is! When we "come home," God is waiting, arms open.

"When he [the son] finally came to his senses..." (Luke 15:17). Have you come to your senses? Have you recognized that there is a God—and it's not you? Has there been a time when a heavenly tug so gripped your heart that you knew unmistakably that God was trying to show you His love through the gift of His Son? If so, what was your response? Was it similar to that of the son in this painting?

I had such a consciousness that God loved and cared for me (John 3:16) that it wasn't difficult to fall into His arms and admit my need for Him.

If you haven't yet returned home to God, how about today? The Prodigal realized that he wasn't even worthy to be called his father's son. We, too, need to understand our unworthiness before a righteous God. The Prodigal depended on his father's mercy. God's mercy through Christ is all we can rely on. When you experience God's welcome, you will really understand this painting.

PAINTER'S NOTES: *The repentant son (us) is in clothing of our time, while the Father (God) is in attire of New Testatment times. Their embrace causes the sun to cast a cross-shaped shadow on the ground. This cross is the only way to the Father. The setting sun symbolizes the lateness of time. The wheat fields represent the harvest Jesus talked about in John 4:35. The houses on the hilltop are neither modern nor from biblical times, indicating that this moment is timeless. A servant runs down the road with a change of clothes for the son. The sun's shape— a dove—reminds us that the Holy Spirit makes this reconciliation possible. The clouds form open arms— God's attitude toward you. He welcomes your neighbors, too—think they'd like to know?*

Come, ye sinners, poor and needy,
Weak and wounded, sick and sore,
Jesus ready stands to save you,
Full of pity, love, and power.

Let not conscience make you linger,
Nor of fitness fondly dream;
All the fitness He requireth
Is to feel your need of Him. —JOSEPH HART (1712–1768)

THOUGHTS FROM THE HEART:

_____
_____
_____
_____
_____
_____
_____
_____

CLEAN

BUT IF WE ARE
LIVING IN THE LIGHT
OF GOD'S PRESENCE,
JUST AS CHRIST IS,
THEN WE HAVE
FELLOWSHIP WITH
EACH OTHER, AND
THE BLOOD OF JESUS,
HIS SON,
CLEANSES US
FROM EVERY SIN.

1 John 1:7

The Cleansing Stream

"los

"all their guilty stains"

William Cowper

In many churches when people decide to commit their lives to Christ, they must "go to the altar." What it means, literally, is the physical sign of your walking forward to accept the atoning work of Calvary to cleanse you from sin and fit you for heaven. Many of us (me included) have met Christ at a church altar. However, asking Christ to come into your heart can happen at home, in your pew at church, or when you're away on vacation. You can be anywhere and recognize that there is only one way to heaven and a right relationship with God. Then you will experience *The Cleansing Stream*.

One time a woman asked me if I would speak to her husband about spiritual things. Awkwardly, I began a conversation that got around to why he doesn't like attending church. He said, "Every time I go, it seems all they want me to do is go to the altar. I'm tired of hearing that." I wasn't prepared to respond at the time. But since then I've considered what the altar means to me. This man may consider "going to the altar" an unwanted experience. But I'm convinced that the day I went to the altar was the day life began for me.

PAINTER'S NOTES: *In the painting I used the metaphor of a waterfall emanating from the cross in the stained-glass window to symbolize the streams of living water Jesus spoke of in John 7:38. We are cleansed of our sins when we repent and ask Christ to come into our heart and take up the proper place of Savior and Lord of our life. There is no other way to obtain it. Not through heredity. Not through association. Only by personal experience. At the altar.*

There is a fountain filled with blood
Drawn from Immanuel's veins;
And sinners, plunged beneath that flood,
Lose all their guilty stains.

E'er since, by faith, I saw the stream
Thy flowing wounds supply,
Redeeming love has been my theme,
And shall be till I die. — WILLIAM COWPER (1731–1800)

THOUGHTS FROM THE HEART:

_____

_____

_____

_____

_____

_____

_____

_____

_____

FAITH

JESUS TURNED AROUND
AND SAID TO HER,
"DAUGHTER,
BE ENCOURAGED!
YOUR FAITH
HAS MADE YOU WELL."
AND THE WOMAN
WAS HEALED
AT THAT MOMENT.

Matthew 9:22

The Touch

"Fai

"...is...God holding...you"

— E. Stanley Jones

Most people would agree that the most pressing spiritual question is: Does God exist? Once we're convinced that God exists, the most critical question must be, Is God accessible to me?

Many of us have heard that God cares and that He answers prayer. We have heard testimonies of His help in time of need. For each of us, though, the only testimony that really counts is our personal one. Is God there in *my* time of need?

One day long ago, a woman had the chance to form her own opinion about that question. She wasn't in a position to casually wait and see. She needed help, and she needed it right away. The Gospel of Luke doesn't say much about this woman's situation except that she had tried everything to get better. Twelve years of trying. Possibly the money was gone, along with her hope that her problem would ever get resolved.

Jesus' reputation must have gone ahead of Him to this woman's town. He was the last possible light at the end of a long tunnel for her. Was it worth a try? Well, we know it was—we have read her story. But when she was in that situation, she didn't know what the outcome would be. Her risk was great. You see, she was touching the hem of *the* High Priest, and she was unclean. If she had been caught, there would have been a penalty to pay. But when you get desperate, reason—and pride—go out the window. Her act of desperation secured her healing—as well as getting her story recorded in the greatest Book of all time! Read Luke 8:43-48.

PAINTER'S NOTES: *The woman in my painting is a contemporary one. She symbolizes our questioning generation. She reaches right past the fancy garments to the One who has the real power—Jesus. He still has that power. But we can only experience it for ourselves when we take the risk and reach out for Him.*

Faith is not merely you holding on to God—it is God holding on to you.

E. STANLEY JONES (1884–1973)

THOUGHTS FROM THE HEART:

_____

_____

_____

_____

_____

_____

_____

_____

_____

PRAYER

SO LET US COME BOLDLY
TO THE THRONE
OF OUR GRACIOUS GOD.
THERE WE WILL
RECEIVE HIS MERCY,
AND WE WILL FIND
GRACE TO HELP US
WHEN WE NEED IT.

Hebrews 4:16

"*lost*

Into His Presence

"our power to visualize"

Oswald Chambers

If there is any habit I would want my children to avoid, it would be the routine of approaching God halfheartedly as though He were a million miles away and hard of hearing. We call it prayer time, but it's more like let-your-mind-wander time. How sad. The King of the universe, the One who formed your body in the womb (Isaiah 49:5) with His own fingers, is the same One who calls you *mine* (Isaiah 43:1). He's also the One who promises to take hold of our hand (Isaiah 42:6) and whose compassions are "new every morning" (Lamentations 3:23, NIV). With assurances like that, you would think we would gladly offer our love and devotion.

One night as my son was saying his nighttime prayers, I noticed he was in the same old rut of "God bless Mommy and Daddy and Grant and . . . ," which is about where I stopped him. I reminded him that Almighty God was waiting to hear him pray. "What is it you want Him to hear?" I asked. He thought for a second and said excitedly, "Oh, OK. Dear God, I thank you for who you are and . . ." and leaped into one of the most beautiful prayers I'd ever heard—from anyone! All it took was a reminder of Who he was about to address. The rest took care of itself.

• • • • •

PAINTER'S NOTES: *First Peter 3:12 says, "For the eyes of the Lord are on the righteous and his ears are attentive to their prayer" (NIV). In the painting the little girl is literally coming into the presence of God. Christ is inviting her in. The angels Isaiah saw (Isaiah 6) are there. Even the dog is aware of the heavenly presence. If Balaam's donkey saw into the angelic dimension (Numbers 22:23), it surely could happen now! If we could begin to capture the magic of that moment we call prayer, we might really change our lives. I've been learning that Disney studios are not the only ones making magical moments. That's why I put the twinkling stars around the room.*

One of the reasons for our sense of futility in prayer is that we have lost our power to visualize. We can no longer even imagine putting ourselves deliberately before God.

OSWALD CHAMBERS (1874–1917)

THOUGHTS FROM THE HEART:

_____

_____

_____

_____

_____

_____

_____

_____

GROWTH

THESE TRIALS ARE ONLY
TO TEST YOUR FAITH,
TO SHOW THAT IT IS
STRONG AND PURE.
IT IS BEING TESTED
AS FIRE TESTS
AND PURIFIES GOLD—
AND YOUR FAITH IS FAR
MORE PRECIOUS TO GOD
THAN MERE GOLD.

1 Peter 1:7

The Chisel

"by

"...through trials God is shaping us"

Growth. You can feel the pain of that word right away. How many times have our children complained of growing pains? We experience growing pains in our spiritual life, too. Growth comes mostly through . . . *pain.*

We often give our children the impression that difficulties are to be avoided at all cost and that difficult circumstances reflect the absence of God in our lives. But just as a sculptor uses a chisel to chip away the rough exterior and get at the beauty underneath, God continually shapes us—through painful times and events—into the image of His Son.

It has been said that when Michelangelo was about to begin sculpting his masterpiece of David, he said, looking at the great block of marble, "David is in there. I must get him out." Somebody terrific is under *our* exterior, and the Master Sculptor can bring him or her to life. We just need to cooperate with the process. He wants us to be works of art in the shape of Christ, and every challenge, every valley, and every moment of pain is a tool in the hands of the Sculptor.

Here is a secret: When you ask for patience, God will usually allow circumstances to help you develop it! The same with courage, peace, trust, and other godly attributes. You can make that process long or short, depending on whether you submit or fight every step of the way. The end of the process? "I will refine them like silver and test them like gold" (Zechariah 13:9, NIV). Looking forward to the gold is my favorite part!

— Henry Ward Beecher

PAINTER'S NOTES: *This painting can be emotionally hard to look at. I show a man in the creation process. Through trials and pains, God is chipping away the rough exterior in order to get at the beauty underneath. I put stars and space as the background because, frankly, it's a supernatural process. When we are going through it, it can feel like we are in another world.*

*We are always in the forge, or on the anvil;
by trials God is shaping us for higher things.*

HENRY WARD BEECHER (1813–1887)

THOUGHTS FROM THE HEART:

_____

_____

_____

_____

_____

_____

_____

_____

HUMILITY

WHOEVER WANTS TO BE
A LEADER AMONG YOU
MUST BE YOUR SERVANT,
AND WHOEVER
WANTS TO BE FIRST
MUST BE THE SLAVE
OF ALL.
FOR EVEN I,
THE SON OF MAN,
CAME HERE NOT
TO BE SERVED
BUT TO SERVE OTHERS,
AND TO GIVE MY LIFE
AS A RANSOM FOR MANY.

Mark 10:43-45

"He．

The Servant

...takes our feet in his hands"

— Max Lucado

Greatness. What a great word! There isn't a parent who doesn't want greatness for his or her child. Where most of us part company is over the way to achieve greatness. If you asked any child to name a great person, he would, more than likely, name a famous athlete, movie star, or rock musician—-at least someone in the public eye. That's what most of us think of as great.

Yet we who are called by Christ's name ought to use *His* definition of greatness. He said a person who chooses to *serve* is great. How many parents will sit at the table this evening and impart that philosophy to their children? In the competitive environment of our world, *should* we encourage our children to become servants? After all, what if they get taken for granted—or taken advantage of?

These questions were answered by the greatest Person of all. He said servanthood *is* the path to greatness. "If anyone wants to be first, he must be the very last, and the servant of all" (Mark 9:35, NIV). It would help if we realized that greatness is in the hand of God. He distributes it as He sees fit. We must only position ourselves—through obedience—to receive it. Then we can relax and watch God's blessing pour into the servant's life.

I couldn't think of a more dramatic way of showing the *opposite* of greatness than a businessman in his office, surrounded by the trappings of success. Surely he's got it made—he's arrived! Not quite. When Christ comes into view, He demonstrates the servant's posture, to the chagrin and humiliation of the man. Just as He did with His own disciples, Christ reminds us of what a great Person looks like. Will we follow His example?

• • • • •

PAINTER'S NOTES: *When this painting was unveiled at a convention some time ago, I was surprised by the comments of people passing by. Many pastors walked by with a spouse or friend and whispered, "Look, there's a pastor in the chair, with Christ washing his feet!" How interesting. They were applying it personally! As always, God did more with the painting than I expected.*

I don't understand how God can be so kind to us, but He is. He kneels before us, takes our feet in His hands, and washes them. Please understand that in washing the disciples' feet, Jesus is washing ours. That's us being cleansed, not from our dirt, but from our sins. — MAX LUCADO, *A Gentle Thunder*

THOUGHTS FROM THE HEART:

_____

_____

_____

_____

_____

_____

_____

_____

_____

ANGELS

PRAISE THE LORD,
YOU ANGELS OF HIS,
YOU MIGHTY CREATURES
WHO CARRY OUT
HIS PLANS,
LISTENING FOR EACH
OF HIS COMMANDS.

Psalm 103:20

FOR THE ANGEL
OF THE LORD GUARDS
ALL WHO FEAR HIM,
AND HE RESCUES THEM.

Psalm 34:7

"ope

...ation of angelic glory,"

— Billy Graham

We can't overestimate the strength of a parent's prayer. Again and again, praying mothers have told me their stories. Sometimes the answer looked a million miles away, but that mother kept praying. And God kept answering. He answered in His time and in His way, but He honored those moments a parent stood before His throne begging for heavenly intervention. Not one prayer goes unheard. Or unanswered.

We would do well to start the process early. We can begin praying for our children while they are still in the womb. It's wise to commit them—and the many facets of their lives—to the Lord long before the moment of birth. I've been praying for years for the wives God will provide for my boys. Before they could walk, I was praying for their careers and that God would use their lives to His glory. I don't think I'll regret that, do you?

I think it's important to pray with the children as part of our family team. We are fond of "agreeing together" in prayer. We're also fond of seeing the answers come. We have documented more miracles than I could have imagined, and we're just getting warmed up! I know the day is coming when Pat and I will be praying alone. Our children will go off to college, get married, move away to a job, and we won't be able to maintain our team prayer time. But they can be sure that I will be praying for them. I promise. It's our covenant, and they can be secure in knowing that God answers a parent's prayer.

PAINTER'S NOTES: *In this painting you see one result of prayer. The angels, though unseen, are promised to us in Scripture (Psalm 34:7). Someday we'll see how much God used them to keep us from the harm and danger of this world. That gives me a lot of comfort when I'm waiting while my sons are out with the car— or in any circumstance that I can't control.*

Christians should never fail to sense the operation of angelic glory. It forever eclipses the world of demonic powers, as the sun does a candle's light. — BILLY GRAHAM (1918–)

THOUGHTS FROM THE HEART:

_____
_____
_____
_____
_____
_____
_____
_____
_____

WARFARE

FOR WE ARE NOT
FIGHTING AGAINST
PEOPLE MADE OF FLESH
AND BLOOD,
BUT AGAINST THE
EVIL RULERS AND
AUTHORITIES OF THE
UNSEEN WORLD,
AGAINST THOSE MIGHTY
POWERS OF DARKNESS
WHO RULE THIS WORLD,
AND AGAINST
WICKED SPIRITS IN THE
HEAVENLY REALMS.

Ephesians 6:12

Spiritual Warfare

"the

"Evil trembles when we pray"

Samuel Chadwick

Countless times I have been asked where I got the idea for this painting. That should be obvious! Ephesians 6:12 is so clear about spiritual warfare. I guess I shouldn't be surprised that we, in the Western world especially, don't want to linger on this concept. It's scary! And the Bible's view of these realities is incompatible with the flood of messages that pervade our society. I don't think we are in much danger of the evening news recognizing the day's events as spiritual warfare! In fact, most people live through their days totally unaware of the great spiritual struggle going on around them, and even inside them. However, those of us who are called Christians know the truth. We also have been given the weapon to fight with: prayer. That's what *Spiritual Warfare* was intended to communicate.

Most people think that the centerpiece of the painting is the angels fighting in the window. It's not. The focus of the painting is the shadow of the cross that's falling on the father and son. Without that as the assurance of our protection, I would be too afraid to approach the subject!

• • • • •

PAINTER'S NOTES: *The father's watch reads almost midnight, indicating the lateness of the "hour." The drapes blow gently from open windows, showing that mere glass or wood will not keep out evil forces. The Noah's ark wallpaper border isn't protection either! Accessorizing our rooms (even with spiritual paintings!) will do nothing if we don't pray. Our enemy would be content to merely have all kinds of righteous "stuff" hanging there— what he doesn't want is prayer. When this painting was near release, people said it would never sell: "Paintings that are powerful just won't make it." When God is directing your steps, you just need to obey. This has proved to be my most popular work.*

The one concern of the devil is to keep Christians from praying. He fears nothing from prayerless studies, prayerless work, and prayerless religion. He laughs at our toil, mocks at our wisdom, but trembles when we pray. — SAMUEL CHADWICK (1832–1917)

THOUGHTS FROM THE HEART:

_____
_____
_____
_____
_____
_____
_____
_____

RAPTURE

TWO MEN WILL BE
WORKING TOGETHER
IN THE FIELD;
ONE WILL BE TAKEN,
THE OTHER LEFT.
TWO WOMEN WILL BE
GRINDING FLOUR
AT THE MILL;
ONE WILL BE TAKEN,
THE OTHER LEFT.
SO BE PREPARED,
BECAUSE YOU
DON'T KNOW WHAT DAY
YOUR LORD IS COMING.

Matthew 24:40-42

The Rapture

"wher

"the world drama will end"

— C. S. Lewis

Nothing scares most children like the thought of being left behind. All of us remember the terrifying experience of getting lost somewhere. Imagine being lost for *eternity*, separated not just from loved ones but from the God who gave us life.

Where will you spend eternity? I think my children have asked me more about "forever" than any other topic, and I'm glad. I'm glad they have already decided to turn to God; the granddaddy of all decisions has been dealt with once and for all. There is a framed piece of paper hanging in each of my children's rooms that tells the day that they asked Jesus Christ to become their personal Lord and Savior. It is a treasured and constant reminder of Who they belong to. Forever. Their names are now written in heaven's book (Revelation 21:27). When Christ returns and "two men will be in the field; one will be taken and the other left" (NIV), I—and they—know they will be taken into the Father's presence.

When I began this painting, I got a lot of resistance from people: "Wouldn't it be improper to give the impression that children could be left?" But how can we know the heart of another person—and at what point God will hold him or her accountable for their sins? Do you want to risk waiting too long to share with your child the forgiveness of God? I hope that some small child, whose heart has begun to understand spiritual realities, will see this painting and understand that he or she can choose to be with God forever.

PAINTER'S NOTES: *The kids in this painting are walking along the road, like on any day. Except this day the dark clouds move in, forming the shape of an angel blowing a trumpet (Matt. 24:31). One child, prepared for that day, rises to meet the Lord, while the other, partially in the dark, is looking down. The shadow of the boy rising forms the shape of the cross, signifying the cost of eternity in heaven. The stars around him symbolize that magical moment of translation.*

The doctrine of the Second Coming teaches us that we do not and cannot know when the world drama will end. The curtain may be rung down at any moment.

C. S. LEWIS (1898–1963)

THOUGHTS FROM THE HEART:

_____
_____
_____
_____
_____
_____
_____
_____
_____

HEAVEN

THERE ARE MANY ROOMS
IN MY FATHER'S HOME,
AND I AM GOING TO
PREPARE A PLACE FOR YOU.
IF THIS WERE NOT SO,
I WOULD
TELL YOU PLAINLY.
WHEN EVERYTHING
IS READY, I WILL COME
AND GET YOU,
SO THAT YOU WILL ALWAYS
BE WITH ME
WHERE I AM.

John 14:2-3

Heaven's Door

"loo

"...looking for a better place"

On October 1, 1971, I came home from the American Academy of Art and found the house empty. I was working on a poster for my church youth group, and I headed toward my worktable in the basement. After a while I needed to get something from the kitchen. That's when I saw the note. My mom had gone to the hospital to be with my dad, who'd had a heart attack at work. He died before she got there.

My last memories of Dad are good ones. A week before he died we were at a church banquet, where we were hugging and affirming our love for each other. My dad had accepted Christ as Savior five years previously.

Sometimes I wonder if those who have gone on before us can see us. (I don't know how all of that works!) Does my dad rejoice at seeing what the Lord is doing with his kid? Is he proud? Sometimes I ask the Lord to relay my love to him, if He sees him that day.

The assurance I have from God's own Word is that we will be reunited someday (John 14:2). I know that I have to make a passage through a doorway for that to happen. I'm ready for that doorway because, like my dad, I accepted Christ as Savior too. When I push back that door, I will be looking for Christ first, then I want to see my dad. And then we'll wait together for my wife (his favorite) and our kids. He'll be delighted to see the grandkids he didn't get a chance to enjoy here.

In this painting the shadows on the door represent the uncertainties we feel on this side of heaven. The weathered door itself shows the wear and tear we experience. I attempted to contrast the dark colors on the door with the magical colors of what's on the other side. A magical Kingdom, prepared just for us!

They were looking for a better place, a heavenly homeland. That is why God is not ashamed to be called their God, for he has prepared a heavenly city for them.

PAUL THE APOSTLE (HEBREWS 11:16)

THOUGHTS FROM THE HEART:

_____
_____
_____
_____
_____
_____
_____
_____
_____

A PAINTER'S STORY

Like the story of the prophet Jeremiah, mine began before I was born. My mother, now eighty-four, tells me that while pregnant, she had decided to terminate the pregnancy. Before the doctor had the chance to begin the procedure, apparently with an injection, she said she heard God "speak" to her, telling her that He had a plan for the baby inside her. She pushed the needle away at the last moment, walked out, and never looked back. While she was not a Christian at the time, my grandmother, who lived with us, was. I have to believe that my grandmother might have been praying from the moment my mother left the house that day.

Throughout my growing years, God began to make my artistic gifts and His calling to use them for Himself clear to me. Once, at a youth evangelistic meeting with probably 1,500–2,000 teens in attendance, the evangelist picked me out from the middle of the auditorium and called me to the front. He asked me if I was aware that God had chosen me. I said yes, wondering how I was to explain this to the other kids on the van ride home.

In 1967, I met a girl who would later become my only date and my wife, now of twenty-five years. Pat kept reminding me of the call for my life and demonstrated her belief in it by giving me my first set of paints and an easel.

In 1970, after high school and one year of college, Pat and I decided to take a leap of faith and enroll me in the American Academy of Art in Chicago. Since my parents could not afford the tuition, Pat and I worked after school to pay the yearly fee. I was a church janitor, while Pat worked at an insurance company. By God's grace, I was accepted into the school. Pat and I agreed to test our decision with a six-month trial period. After six months, the instructors applauded my hard work and invested themselves in me. (I will always be particularly grateful for the years I spent under the teaching of Bill Parks, who to this day continues to monitor my career.) Pat and I decided I should stay for the three-year course.

God honored our decision with heavenly help, since it was shortly after this that my father died. I was called into the office about a week later and was told by the president of the school, watercolorist Irving Shapiro, that someone had donated money to the school, and they wanted to apply it to my next year's education. I thanked him in light of what had happened to my dad, feeling that his gracious offer was out of sympathy, to which he replied, "I didn't know your father had passed away." Looking back, I realize that God was providing a way to keep his plan for me on track.

EARLY SUCCESSES

In my first year, one of my instructors who was a Christian shocked me when I told him that someday I would devote my talents to the Christian community in hopes of being involved in a second Renaissance. His response was, "It will never happen." He explained that, in his view, the Church was uninterested in aesthetics and that there would be no budget or support for my art there. I would be better off taking my talents to the secular industry (ad agencies and such).

For the next eighteen years, I found out, sadly, that my instructor was right. The Church had no apparent interest in using art for anything more than decoration. My career consequently went in the secular direction and prospered beyond my wildest dreams. Although I had agents in Chicago, I had the privilege of acquiring the Leff Agency to represent me in New York. God blessed me with this husband-and-wife team who were very devoted to me and to this day remain friends. (Thank you, Jerry and Wilma. You will always hold a special place in my heart.) Through their representation, I began doing paintings for some of the world's largest and best-known companies.

I was awarded the honor of being the official illustrator for the Moscow Olympics in 1980. The agency that hired me for the work came to Chicago to pick up the painting and told me that "99 percent of America will know your name after this." Surely this was God, I thought. A few months later, as Pat and I were watching television, a news bulletin interrupted the program and President Jimmy Carter announced that the United States would boycott the Olympics because of international human-rights issues.

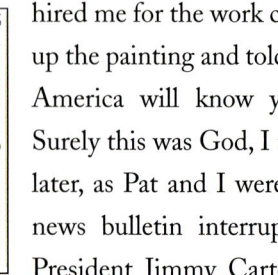

Pat and I sat there in total shock and disbelief. That was to be my year, and that's not exactly what I had in mind! But we later found out that God is in even the seeming reversals of our lives. Had the Olympics gone through, I would almost certainly have chosen a different road and missed God's plan for me. I must admit, I couldn't see that at the time, but that's why I have come to regard Proverbs 3:5-6 as one of my life verses: "Trust in the Lord with all your heart and lean not on your own understanding; in all your ways acknowledge him, and he will make your paths straight" (NIV). My career continued, and my work was now starting to travel internationally and mounting more than I could have ever believed.

While I was certainly pleased with my success, there was always a longing to do what I had known was placed in my heart twenty years earlier. That passion had not abated. Little did I know that all of the work I was doing was merely the training ground for what was to come. Ten years ago, that all changed for me.

A CLEAR CALL

In one of my quiet times before the Lord, I distinctly heard His "still small voice" saying that now was the time I had been waiting for. Since I was so consumed with prior commitments—and a little stunned to suddenly hear God say, "Now!"—I made a feeble attempt to move in that direction. In fact, I responded with a casual request: Would He put the plan together (in a big way, of course) so that I could step in at my convenience? My personal observation on obeying God's call: If ever things are going too well for you and you would like that to change, then, by all means, give God the response I did, and things will certainly change! God humbled me and brought me to my knees in repentance. When I came back to my knees in the spirit of obedience and servanthood (about two months later), I told God that I was willing to do anything He wanted. (That was the pain talking, you realize!) Nevertheless, I was ready for marching orders.

Then God impressed the thought on me: *What if it isn't even you I am choosing for this Renaissance?* I came back to my knees and asked the Lord to at least give me the privilege of ringing the doorbell of the one He had chosen, and I would bring his artwork back. God gently spoke to my heart and told me that I was the one but that I was not the only one He was choosing.

Since that time I have spent years doing all I could to disciple other excellent Christian artists who are successful in the secular market. One of the fruits of that commitment was the MasterPeace Collection, which I cofounded and oversaw for a number of years. Our new company named Art2See is an expansion of that original vision God had given me.

I believe that Scripture is filled with enough creative and imaginative eternal subject matter to keep an artist or filmmaker busy for many lifetimes. One of my favorite verses to fuel my creative juices is John 21:25: "Jesus did many other things as well. If every one of them were written down, I suppose that even the whole world would not have room for the books that would be written" (NIV).

To my dismay, I have not always sensed that the Church is convinced that God is in favor of the arts as a legitimate way to communicate the things of God. I am comforted when I read Exodus 31:1-6, which records God's desire for the arts in His tabernacle. "Then the Lord said to Moses, 'See, I have chosen Bezalel son of Uri, the son of Hur, of the tribe of Judah, and I have filled him with the Spirit of God, with skill, ability and knowledge in all kinds of crafts—to make artistic designs for work in gold, silver and bronze, to cut and set stones, to work in wood, and to engage in all kinds of craftsmanship. Moreover, I have appointed Oholiab son of Ahisamach, of the tribe of Dan, to help him. Also I have given skill *to all the craftsmen* to make everything I have commanded you" (NIV, emphasis mine). It makes sense that the Author of creativity can impart that to His children. In Ephesians 2:10 we are called God's "poems" *(poeima)*. Imagine God using an artistic term for His own creating!

WHAT IT'S GOING TO TAKE

In the Renaissance, the arts were effectively used by the Church. Because the Church was the major producer of art in society, godly messages pervaded that society. *God was visually declared with each work of art.*

Look around today. Can you think of a society that could use a dose of that more than ours? Experts say that sight and sound have become preferred means of learning, apart from entertaining us. Isn't it time we saturate our society with messages worth seeing and hearing? Dr. Calvin Seervald said, "Whatever arena Christians withdraw from goes to Hell." The arts for the most part have. We need a second Renaissance. This certainly is one of the untapped resources to fulfill Mark 16:15, where Jesus commanded us to go into all the world and preach the gospel.

In order to spread the Good News through art, we need to honor some foundational principles.

Passion for the mission and our world's needs. Christian artists often ask me what they are supposed to paint, hoping for a "marketing" clue to good sales. I answer with this question: "What makes you weep when you are on your knees before God? That is what you are supposed to address in your work!" N. C. Wyeth said, "You can only paint out of conviction." After my first two decades of painting for money, I have found this to be true.

Excellence. I believe that if you have been gifted with artistic ability, you are responsible to develop it to the fullest. Anything less for the Author of Excellence is not acceptable. In fact, I believe that many times the gospel is rejected, not because of its content, but because of its poor presentation!

The right focus. I believe that painters and every other kind of artist have a choice when executing the finished piece. They can either cause you to focus on *what* they painted or on *how* they painted it. They cannot do both with equal power. It has often been said that Norman Rockwell (one of my favorites) always caused you to see what he painted, instead of how great his craftsmanship or technique was. It would be rare for a person to view *Doctor and Doll* or *Saying Grace* and be more struck by the fancy brushwork or creative use of composition than by the emotion of the scene.

Similarly, I hope that my work will make you look, but more important, make you *see!* As a speaker aims to *tell* you the truth, I aim to *show* you the truth. Recently a kind lady said, "Do you know what I consider you are doing in your work? I think God is using you to give us another translation of the Bible! Just as we have different versions of Scripture, you are putting it in a visual translation!" I nearly fell off my chair. May it be so, under God's perfect timing!

It is my hope that as you read this book, your view of God will be as lofty as He deserves and that His presence will be closer to you than ever before.

Please pray for me and all artists when you can.

P.S. At an appearance of my work in 1996, an older man came up to greet me. I was shocked to see that it was the same instructor I mentioned earlier in this writing. I asked him if he remembered our conversation twenty-six years before. He said he did, and we embraced, a little choked up at what God is doing in my life!

"THE CHRISTIAN
IS THE ONE
WHOSE
IMAGINATION
SHOULD FLY
BEYOND
THE STARS"

Francis Schaeffer